T0354452

Sugar Shack

Joyce M. Poindexter Bush

Illustrations by Sonny Heston

AuthorHouse™ LLC
1663 Liberty Drive
Bloomington, IN 47403
www.authorhouse.com
Phone: 1-800-839-8640

Published by AuthorHouse   09/18/2014

ISBN: 978-1-4969-4076-6 (sc)
ISBN: 978-1-4969-4077-3 (hc)
ISBN: 978-1-4969-4075-9 (e)

Library of Congress Control Number: 2014916585

Events in our lives help to shape who we are.

Much love and appreciation to my family and friends who have helped me to understand that "All things work together for good, for those who love the Lord and are called according to **His Purpose**."

Romans 8:28

Contents

Contents

CHAPTER 1

Pinky Promise

The last time Catherine spent the night at my house, the Sugar Shack caught on fire. I can see it now, the little, two-room, yellow and white house that Daddy built on the front edge of our acre lot, all ablaze. That's where Mama cooked and sold her homemade candy. I told Daddy that bright colors made it easy for people to see the shack from a distance. Mama and Daddy always liked my suggestions. That's why I felt that they loved and appreciated me. Maybe too much. They always complimented me on my positive outlook on things, so I always tried to do what I thought would please them. Looking at the burned shack, I knew I had to do something to help.

People would come from far and near to buy Mama's taffy and jelly-filled hard candies. Catherine and I always cleaned up the cozy little kitchen after the candy store closed. We liked making the silver plated appliances shine like a mirror, because they were in the same room where the customers stood to buy the candy. Many times, the people complimented Mama on how cozy and clean the candy store was.

1

"Thanks to my daughter and her friend," Mama would say.

The back room of the shack was my 'hang-out' spot. The metal cabinets that were lined against one wall, looked like tall, thin soldiers preparing to march into battle. They were used for storing supplies and ingredients for making the candy. I remember that a shipment of thirty, five pound bags of sugar had been delivered on the day of the fire.

Catherine and I had helped Daddy stack the bags on the counter in the back until he could make space for them in one of the cabinets.

After cleaning the kitchen on that unforgettable day, Catherine and I sat at the little table in the back room enjoying some of Mama's chocolate taffy.

"Gwen," Mama had said as she and Daddy prepared to go back up to the house, "Don't stay down here too long. We don't want to use too much electricity. The bill is getting pretty high."

"Okay Mama," I replied with a mouthful of taffy.

By the way, my name is Gwendolyn, Gwendolyn Cole. My family and friends call me Gwen.

I recall thinking how quickly the sun set that evening. It set faster than Mama and Daddy could get back to the house.

"I'll light a candle and turn off the light," I remember telling Catherine. "Then we can stay out here longer."

"That's a good idea," Catherine said. "I like how your parents trust you. They don't nag you like my parents do."

"Yeah," I said, "I'm their perfect child."

We laughed and ate more taffy.

"And you and I are perfect friends," I added. "Let's promise to be friends forever."

I held out my pinky finger. Catherine quickly hooked her pinky around mine.

"Pinky promise?" I asked.

"Pinky promise," Catherine replied with confidence.

Funny how I can remember that conversation as if it happened yesterday. The warm evening air whispered gently through the tall trees near the little shack. The night sky sparkled with a billion dancing stars. By the time we had decided to go back up to the house, Catherine was afraid to walk in the dark, so she picked up the candle to give us some light. I checked the front door to make sure it was locked, but we went out the back door because Catherine said it was closer to the house. The lock in the back door sometimes got stuck and it was hard to turn the key. Of all times, that night was one of those 'sometimes'.

I remember taking the candle from Catherine because she was moving the light so much I couldn't see what I was doing.

I finally locked the door, and just in time, too. A big gust of wind came and blew out the light on that short, fat candle. Catherine got so scared she ran to the house without me. In my haste, I jerked the key out of the lock, lost by balance and fell backwards to the ground. The candle fell out of my hand. I scrambled around on the ground trying to find it.

Catherine was yelling from the front porch, "Come on, Gwen!"

I saw a spark near the dry bushes next to the shack, but I decided that since I didn't see any more sparks or smoke, the candle must be completely out. I ran to the house so Catherine could stop yelling.

"I dropped the candle," I kept whispering to Catherine, almost out of breath.

She assured me that everything should be okay because the wind had already blown out the flame. I don't know why I listened to her that night, but I remember thinking what a relief to be inside and getting ready for bed. We lounged in our pajamas and talked 'girl talk'. You know, about boys and stuff. I figured that would get the candle off of our minds. We talked about the boys that lived next door. I said I would marry Mark and Catherine would marry James. We continued to talk until we both, finally, drifted off to sleep.

At about one o'clock in the morning, we were startled awake by Daddy's loud voice, "FIRE! Fire down at the Sugar Shack!"

Frantically, we grabbed our robes and slippers and stood looking out of the window. Flames were shooting up from the back of the shack. Mama and Daddy were unrolling the water hose as the neighborhood volunteers came in the old firetruck. The siren squealed like the sound of howling coyotes. Catherine sat down on the bed nervously rubbing her ankle. I don't think she could bear to watch. The volunteers quickly put out the fire and checked to make sure there was no gas leak.

Daddy said the bags of sugar were destroyed and the back wall and part of the floor would have to be replaced.

Mama saw Catherine rubbing her ankle.

"Are you alright?" I remember Mama asking.

"I twisted my ankle running up the steps from the Sugar Shack," Catherine answered.

Mama was a pretty good nurse. She carefully wrapped a towel with ice around Catherine's ankle and propped her leg up on a pillow.

"I'll call your parents early in the morning to let them know what happened," Mama said assuredly.

As we crawled back into bed, I remember hearing Daddy tell Mama that it was the smell of wax and smoke that woke him up.

Catherine had gone back to sleep, but I sat in bed knowing that the candle I dropped must have started the fire.

I thought to myself, I won't tell Mama and Daddy and I never will. They think I'm their perfect child. If Catherine hadn't been here, this never would have happened.

I wanted to be angry with her, but I remembered our 'pinky promise', *Friends Forever.*

Catherine seemed to be hopping a little when she went home the next morning. She lives about eighteen miles outside of Warren. She and I didn't say much to each other when she left. We didn't even wave when her mother's old, gray truck backed out of the driveway. I saw Catherine glance at the burned shack.

I wondered if she felt it was her fault?

I certainly did!

CHAPTER 2

Playing Church

D addy said it was going to take a while to get the Sugar Shack back to normal.

"Money is tight," he said. "And my little retirement doesn't go very far."

I didn't realize how much Mama's candy sales were helping us. The more I thought about that candle, the more I realized I needed to help right away. But, what could I do? I couldn't even go near the shack. Daddy said it wasn't safe.

"Sunday morning! Time to get up!" Mama bellowed.

I didn't feel very righteous. In fact, I felt guilty. I hadn't talked to Catherine since the fire, and Mama and Daddy would probably begin to wonder why I hadn't invited her over for the weekend.

"What can I possibly tell them?" I whispered to myself.

I picked the brightest colored dress in my closet to wear to church.

Maybe this yellow dress will camouflage how I feel, I thought.

I had just finished combing my hair when the telephone rang.

"Hello Mark," I heard Mama say. "You need a ride to church?"

Mama and Daddy were always helpful to our neighbors.

"Mark is on his way over!" Mama yelled.

Mama knew I kind of liked Mark, but today, I didn't really want to be bothered. I was pretty tired from tossing and turning all night, thinking about what I could do to fix the Sugar Shack.

I hope he doesn't ask me anything about the Sugar Shack, I thought to myself.

As I opened the curtains in my room, I saw Mark walking around the Shack.

What is he looking at? I thought with disgust. Just come on to the door.

As Mark walked near the back of the shack, I saw him pick up something from the bushes. My heart sank at the thought of him finding the candle I dropped. What ever it was, he wrapped it in a tissue and put it in his jacket pocket.

"It was Catherine's fault," I kept telling myself. "Yes, it was her fault that the Sugar Shack burned."

For some reason, today, my words didn't seem very convincing.

I sat in the back seat of the car next to Mark.

"I like your yellow dress," he said.

I told him all about how Mama made it for me. I talked all the way to church so no one else would have a chance to say anything. I didn't want anyone to mention anything about the fire.

Church was packed today. Mama sang in the choir and Daddy ushered, so I squeezed onto the third row next to Mrs. Simmons. Mark had to sit on the second row because he is a Junior Deacon in training.

The music was very lively, as always, and the sermon was exceptionally motivating. People were jumping and shouting up and down the aisles. To my surprise, Mark jumped up and shouted in the aisle, too. His jacket bobbed up and down as he praised with his arms straight up. The ball of tissue fell from his pocket.

Was it the candle? I thought.

I had to get whatever it was, so I got up and began to jump up and down in the aisle too, until I spotted the tissue. I stooped down and picked it up, pretending to shout back to my seat. I put it in my purse and sat quietly for the rest of the service.

When church was over, Mark rode home with one of the head deacons. I couldn't wait to get home to see what Mark had dropped.

"Church was good, wasn't it?" Daddy said. "They really worked the ushers today."

"Yeah," Mama responded, "I haven't seen that many people up shouting in a long time. Sometimes, when that many people get up, it makes you wonder if some of them aren't just faking."

"You mean *playing church*?" I chimed in.

"Yeah," Mama replied.

I looked down at my purse, "Lord, forgive me," I whispered softly.

I went straight to my room when we got home. Mama and Daddy never intruded on my privacy. My hands shook and my heart beat rapidly as I quickly unwrapped the object. Inside the tissue was a smooth, oval-shaped rock.

What is so important about this rock? I wondered.

Oh, well, at least it's not the candle.

I put the rock in my dresser drawer as I admired my dress in the mirror.

"I look nice in yellow," I said out loud as if I was actually talking to someone.

"Mark said he liked my yellow dress. I hope that means he likes me, too."

I smiled and turned around like a little kid trying to be a ballerina.

"I'll give Mark his rock tomorrow."

I hung my dress in the closet and put on my faded jeans and light blue t- shirt. Daddy and I enjoyed sitting in the old wooden swing on the front porch on Sundays while Mama cooked. Her fried chicken cooking on a Sunday afternoon always seemed to smell so heavenly. Mama had made homemade ice cream, too. Daddy's job was to turn the crank until the cream was frozen. I liked putting the ice and rock salt around the metal pot in the wooden ice cream freezer and watching Daddy crank until the handle wouldn't move anymore.

"That's when you know the cream is frozen and ready to eat," He explained.

He and I gently scooped some ice cream out with our fingers.

"Now that's good ice cream," Daddy said. "Your mother makes the best ice cream this side of the Mississippi."

I knew that was a catchy phrase that people used, to express when they thought something was super great, the absolute best.

"Hey!" I shouted, "Maybe we can sell Mama's ice cream until the shack is fixed. We can sell it right here from the front porch."

"Not a bad idea," Daddy replied.

CHAPTER 3

Magic Wanda

Ms. Wanda was 82 years old. She didn't have a home of her own, so she just went from house to house in our neighborhood and stayed with whomever would let her. Mama and Daddy always welcomed her with open arms. Sometimes Ms. Wanda would stay with us for three or four weeks at a time. She stayed with us so much until I began calling her Aunt Wanda.

"Here comes Aunt Wanda, Mama," I called.

"Check her room Gwen, and put some clean towels in her bathroom," Mama said.

I helped Aunt Wanda up the front porch steps and put her small bag of clothes and other belongings in her room.

"Would you like some ice cream?" Mama asked as she gave Aunt Wanda a big hug.

"Don't mind if I do," Aunt Wanda responded graciously.

Mama handed her a paper cup of ice cream with a plastic spoon.

Aunt Wanda loved ice cream. In fact, she loved to eat. She weighed about 200 pounds, which really showed because she was not very tall.

"Margaret," Aunt Wanda called to my mom, "This ice cream is the best I've had since I was here the last time."

Mama laughed, but I had an idea.

I put my yellow dress back on and asked Daddy for permission to take Mark his rock. He told me I could. As I passed several neighbors on the way, I told them about Mama's ice cream.

"One dollar a cup! Spread the word," I said. "Just go to our porch. Ms. Wanda is sitting there."

Everyone knew Ms. Wanda.

I knocked on Mark's door. He came out on his porch smiling as I gave him the rock.

"I was wondering what happened to this," he said.

"What's so important about this rock?" I asked.

"Oh, I'm a rock collector. I keep rocks that look unusual or special to me," he explained, appearing to blush.

Maybe he's not telling the truth, I thought.

"Would you like to help me sell my Mama's ice cream?" I asked.

"Sure," Mark grinned. "I don't have anything else to do today."

By the time we got back to my porch, people were lined up to buy Mama's ice cream. I quickly explained my idea to Mama and Daddy and they were very pleased. Daddy got his money box and Mama began scooping ice cream into the paper cups. Mark and I took the orders and gave out the ice cream while Daddy took the money. Aunt Wanda sat in the swing humming an old gospel tune. People stood around the porch eating ice cream and enjoying Aunt Wanda's tune. Then her humming turned into singing with words. The louder she sang, the more the people came. Some people even bought seconds.

"Aunt Wanda is like magic," I told Mark.

"She surely is," he replied.

He and I shared a soft laugh together.

"How is your friend Catherine?" Mark asked. "I haven't heard you mention her name in a while."

I looked at Mark in surprise.

The last person I wanted to talk about was Catherine, and what made him think about her anyway?

"I think she's been pretty busy lately, but she was here a few weeks ago." I mumbled.

"Yeah, I saw her from a distance when I was out in my yard," Mark said with a smile.

I didn't want to talk about Catherine anymore so I began singing with Aunt Wanda.

It was getting late but people were still standing around, even after the ice cream was gone. Mark finally went home, tossing and catching his special rock on the way. I stood watching him until he was out of sight.

"I'll be back to help tomorrow," Mark had said before he left.

School was out for the summer, so Mama, Daddy and I stayed up late making ice cream for the next day. Aunt Wanda went to bed. She was tired from all of her 'magical' singing.

"This was a wonderful idea, Gwen!" Daddy exclaimed as he counted the money. "We made over two hundred dollars today! Thanks to you, I can start repairing the Sugar Shack."

I was so happy to know that my idea helped. I made some fliers to advertise Mama's ice cream business. Daddy said he would post some in the hardware store and several other stores in town.

The next morning Mark came to help as he said. My yellow dress made a nice, colorful outfit for selling Mama's ice cream. We had just sat down to eat breakfast, so Mama invited Mark to join us. He didn't hesitate because he hadn't eaten breakfast at home.

"I really love pancakes," he said.

Aunt Wanda put four cakes on his plate. He doused them with butter and warm maple syrup.

"Mmm, I could eat here every morning," he said joyfully as he shoved a mound of pancakes into his mouth.

Mama and Daddy looked at me and smiled.

I thought about the special rock.

"What did you do with your special rock?" I asked inquisitively.

"Oh, I put it with the rest of my collection," Mark answered.

"May I have a glass of water?" he quickly asked Mama.

I could tell he didn't want to talk about it anymore.

Magic Wanda patted him on the shoulder.

"You're a very nice young man," she said. "I'm sure your family is very proud of you."

Mark looked down at his plate. He just smiled and took the last bite of his breakfast. Aunt Wanda helped Mama clean up the kitchen. I missed cleaning the appliances in the Sugar Shack, and deep down inside, I was beginning to miss Catherine, too.

Mark and I cleaned the porch and got everything prepared for the day. I was careful not to get my dress dirty. Daddy was getting ready to go and buy lumber to start working on the Sugar Shack. I reminded him to pass out the fliers.

"Sure thing, Gwen," grinned Daddy. "You're the boss."

He lovingly gave me a pat on the head.

Aunt Wanda came out and sat in the rocking chair Daddy had put on the porch for her. Daddy asked Mark to go with him to get the lumber.

Mark was always very polite.

"Yes sir, Mr. Cole," Mark said. "I'll go and help you."

"Sure is nice to have friends," Aunt Wanda said, as I sat on the step in the bright, shining sun next to her chair. "It's no fun being alone."

I thought about Catherine and the fun we had together. Aunt Wanda knew Catherine because she had been at our house sometimes when Catherine would come to spend the night.

"Mark is my new friend," I quickly said. "And I think he likes me."

"My mama used to tell me," Aunt Wanda said, "Never burn bridges."

"What does that mean, Aunt Wanda?" I asked.

"Child, that means be careful who you cut out of your life and why, because you never know when you might need them back."

Aunt Wanda had a special gift. She could always sense when something was wrong and I felt comfortable talking to her. She really was like magic. I didn't even have to tell her what happened between Catherine and I, and 'Magic Wanda' didn't ask.

CHAPTER 4

See, That's What You Get

Daddy mentioned several times how dangerous going near the burned shack could be. But, while he and Mark were in town, I decided to search for the candle or some melted wax. I thought I might be able to find something before Daddy started repairing things.

The tall weeds that had grown up around the shack tickled my face as I bent down to search in the area where I remember seeing the spark. There was no sign of the candle at all. I searched all around, but found nothing.

Disappointed, I stood up to go back to the porch. Just then, Daddy and Mark were pulling into the driveway with the lumber. When Daddy saw me by the shack, he jumped out of the truck.

"Gwen," he said in a stern voice, "Come away from that shack! I told you it's too dangerous!"

I've never seen Daddy so upset. In my haste, I turned quickly to run away from the shack. My yellow dress got caught on one of the nails that stuck out from the plastic Daddy had put over the back room. My beautiful dress ripped as I jerked away and ran, nonstop, to my room.

Mark saw the whole incident. I was so embarrassed. Who can I talk to now? Mama and Aunt Wanda were preparing to sell the ice cream. Mark and Daddy were unloading the truck and there I sat, all alone, in my torn dress. I thought about what Aunt Wanda had said. You know, about burning bridges.

I changed my clothes and decided to call Catherine. I checked with Mama to make sure it was okay to invite her over. It had never been a problem before, but I didn't want to take the chance of Mama getting upset with me, too.

Catherine was happy to hear from me. Her Mother said she could spend the night. I could hardly wait for her to get here. I cleaned my room and put fresh towels on Catherine's bed. I put my torn dress in a paper bag and sat it on the floor in my closet.

The thought of going out and facing Mark and Daddy made me very sad, but I had to help Mama sell the ice cream, especially since it was my idea.

I hesitantly walked out to the front porch. People were already lined up buying ice cream. Mark was helping Mama, and Daddy was already taking the money. Magic Wanda sang her gospel songs as usual. More and more people joined the line. I tried not to show my sadness, so I smiled and went right to work helping Mark take the orders.

It didn't take long for Catherine to come. When her parent's truck pulled into the driveway, Catherine didn't jump out as usual. In fact, she got out very slowly. Her mother carried her overnight bag as Catherine hobbled around the front of the truck. She was wearing a cast on her left leg.

I gasped, "Catherine, your leg!"

Mark ran over and took the bag from her mother. I had to keep taking orders and passing out cups of ice cream. Mark helped Catherine up the steps and got a chair for her to sit in. I admire how he's thoughtful like that.

"I'll take my bag," Catherine smiled and said to Mark. "I have something special in it."

Catherine's mother thanked Mama for doctoring on Catherine's leg when she was here.

"Accidents do happen," Catherine's mother said kindly.

Mama said Catherine and I could enjoy each others company and she and Daddy would finish selling the ice cream. I wasn't sure what to say to Catherine about the fire. I knew I had to tell her something before she mentioned the candle in front of Mama and Daddy.

Mark stood with his hands behind his back, shifting from one foot to the other as if he didn't know whether he should stay or go home. Just then his brother, James, came running across the yard to our porch.

"Hey Mark! Got to go! Dad's here to pick us up."

Mark didn't look very happy.

"Well, I guess I have to go," he said. "Bye Catherine, bye Gwen, I'll see you tomorrow. How long are you going to be here, Catherine?" Mark asked, as he and his brother began walking away.

"I'll be leaving tomorrow night," Catherine replied.

"Oh, tomorrow night," Mark grinned.

He couldn't stop looking at Catherine. I didn't know what that was all about.

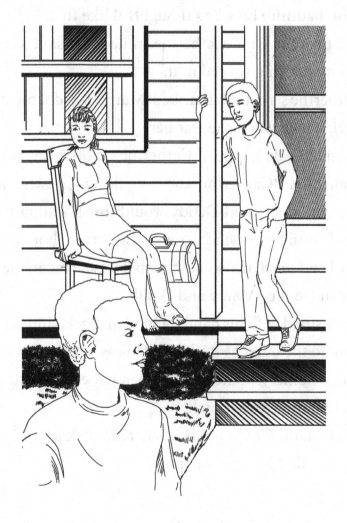

"Come on, Mark, let's go!" yelled James.

"I'm coming. I'm coming." Mark said reluctantly.

I helped Catherine into the house and to my room. I couldn't help but feel a little jealous of her pink cast with her pink and white dress. Her wavy black hair was pulled back into a ponytail. Her pink and black butterfly hair clamp adorned her hair like she was a fashion model.

Catherine began to talk as she sat on the bed.

"I brought you a gift, Gwen. I felt badly about the Sugar Shack fire. I think it was my fault."

Catherine pulled out a pretty, pink flashlight with my name engraved on the side.

"Now when we sit in the shack after dark, we won't have to use a candle," Catherine said quietly with a smile.

"Thank you, Catherine," I said as I gave her my biggest, warmest hug.

I didn't even have to tell her that I thought the fire was her fault, too.

"Did you tell your parents that we had a candle that night?" Catherine asked.

"No!" I exclaimed. "I don't want them to be disappointed in me. I can't believe we made that terrible mistake."

"It was an accident, Gwen. I don't know of anyone who doesn't make a mistake or two now and then. Don't you remember what our summer camp leader said last year?"

"You can't go through life feeling that you always have to be perfect."

Catherine patted me on the shoulder. "You'll be a messed up, nervous wreck trying to hide the things you do that might not be right."

Catherine made a lot of sense and I realized that she had been a better friend to me than I had been to her. The pause in our conversation gave me time to think about my friendship with her.

"What really happened to your leg?" I asked Catherine, feeling pretty guilty.

"That night, when I ran back to the house in the dark, I twisted my ankle and fell going up the steps. That's what really happened. I didn't know my ankle was broken until my mom took me to the hospital the next day."

I wanted to say, "See, that's what you get." But I looked at my pink flashlight and remembered her friendship to me.

I have to be a better friend. Yes, and I will, I thought to myself.

Catherine took a black, permanent marker out of her bag.

"Gwen," she said with a smile, "You can be the first to sign my cast."

I drew a small, arched bridge and wrote the word 'me' at one end and 'you' at the other end. Under the bridge, I wrote 'friends forever'. Catherine really liked it. I'm glad she did.

CHAPTER 5

The Parade

Mama's ice cream was selling almost faster than she could make it.

Whenever Daddy counted the money, he would say, "Wow, we're cooking with Crisco."

I knew that meant we had made a lot of money. Catherine and I were up early the next morning. Mark was an early riser, too. I was hoping he would come early enough to eat breakfast with us again. Mama was making fried apples, bacon and biscuits. Mmm, my favorite.

I heard music coming from the kitchen. Daddy had fixed the old radio he had bought at a yard sale. It sounded pretty good to have only cost $2.50.

Catherine sat down at the table as I tapped my toes and shook my hips like a hula dancer.

Mama laughed and said, "Go on girl!"

I spun around and took a bow. Catherine clapped like she was at a show.

"Where's Aunt Wanda?" I asked Mama. "She likes to watch me dance."

"Ms. Wanda left very early this morning. She went to stay with Mrs. Bell for a while," Mama said.

"Aw," I pouted, "I didn't even get to say bye."

"She'll be back before you know it. You know how Ms. Wanda is," Mama chuckled.

As we finished our breakfast, Catherine said, "I loved the fried apples, Mrs. Margaret."

"I'll bet Mark would have liked them, too," I chimed in.

"Oh, I didn't tell you," Mama said. "There was a big oil spill on the main highway, so the road will be closed until late tonight."

"I guess Mark won't be coming today," Catherine said sadly.

I stared at Catherine for what seemed to be an eternity.

I think Catherine might like Mark, I thought. I hope I'm wrong.

"I'd better call my mother," Catherine said. "I'll probably need to stay another night."

"That would be fine Catherine," Mama said. "You know you are welcome here any time. The County Fair starts tomorrow down at Carter's Field. A big parade on Madison Street will be the opening event. You can go with us!"

"That would be fun," I forced myself to say.

But really, I felt that Catherine just wanted to stay to see Mark.

Seems like something is always interfering with our friendship. Maybe I was just making something out of nothing. I'd have to wait and see.

People excitedly lined the street early the next day for the parade. We were a little late because Catherine couldn't walk very fast. Her doctor put a rubber piece at the bottom of her cast for her to walk on. I'm glad she didn't have crutches because that probably would have made her walk even slower. Daddy found a spot near Carter's Field where he could park the truck and we could watch the parade. That's where the parade was supposed to end. Daddy put two lawn chairs along the street for Mama and Catherine. He let the back of the truck down and he and I sat there eating the peanuts that he brought from home. I'm glad Daddy and I sat together. He gave me a big hug, which is something he didn't do very often.

"Gwen," he said, "I want you to know how proud I am of you. You're not perfect, but you do try hard. Keep up the good work."

"Thanks Daddy," I said.

I decided then, that I should tell him about the fire and the candle I dropped. I figured he wouldn't yell in front of all of the parade watchers.

"You didn't start that fire, Gwen," Daddy said. "The fireman said the fire started from the inside of the shack. There must have been a shortage in the electrical wiring."

"But you said you smelled wax that night," I reminded Daddy.

"That must have been the melted sugar, I guess," Daddy said.

I was so relieved, I reached up and patted Daddy's bald head.

"You're the best Dad in the whole wide world," I said with a smile.

"The parade's coming!" Catherine shouted.

I jumped off of the truck and ran to the edge of the street by Catherine's chair. We saw Mark running along the side of the street coming towards us.

"Hello everybody," he said out of breath. "I've been looking all over for you."

"Hi Mark," we all said as he stood next to me. Sweat ran down his face as he rubbed his hands together nervously. The smell of popcorn and cotton candy filled the air. The music and drumming from the marching band made our hearts pound. We clapped our hands and waved as the participants passed by. High stepping drum majors, clanging cymbals to John Phillip Sousa songs, juggling clowns, decorated cars, and to top it all off, for the first time, there were two stilt-walkers. They were escorted by four African drummers dressed in red, green and black costumes. The stilt-walkers wore Kente cloth vests, raffia skirts and gold and green pants that matched their long-sleeved shirt. Their faces were covered with decorated African masks and they danced with unbelievable skills on the stilts. They jumped, kicked their legs up and even twirled around to the beat of the drums.

"I've never seen anything like this!" Mama exclaimed in awe. "I wonder who they are?"

They came and stood in the street right in front of us. Catherine's eyes were as big as marbles. Mark kept looking and laughing at her. One stilt-walker threw a hand full of candy to us. I ran around picking up so much candy, it barely fit in my pockets. When I returned to the sidewalk, Catherine was standing up. She said that the stilt-walker gave her a beautiful painted rock.

"Let me see it!" I screamed, as the last group of performers loudly marched by.

There was a red heart and some yellow stars on one side and the letter 'W' painted on the other.

"This is gorgeous," I said. "Do you want me to keep it in my pocket for you?"

I gave Mark some of the candy. Catherine gave me the rock since she didn't have any pockets.

"Don't lose it," she smiled.

Mark said he had to go and find his brother. Catherine and I watched as he jogged away.

"He's cute," Catherine said.

I quickly agreed, "Yeah, he's really cute."

Catherine turned and folded up her chair as if she hadn't heard me. Daddy loaded everything into the truck and he and Mama said they would meet us later. Catherine and I walked slowly around the fairgrounds. Trying to be a good friend is pretty hard, but I was determined I wasn't going to let anything mess up my day. I tried not to think about the rock, the twinkle in Catherine's eyes as she watched Mark, or her 'cute' comment. I shared the candy in my pocket with her. We couldn't ride on anything because of her cast, but we looked at the pretty things for sale and played some of the games.

Catherine wanted to play the 'Throw the Dart' game.

"Three tries," the guy said.

The prizes were live goldfish in plastic bags. The bags were lined up along the ledge just below the inflated balloons on the game board.

"Just throw the darts, burst one balloon and you'll win a goldfish," said the guy in charge. Catherine picked up three darts. She aimed for the red balloon and threw one dart. It stuck in the board between two balloons. Her second throw went pretty much the same way.

"One more try, Catherine. Make it a good one," I grinned.

She aimed and threw hard. The dart hit one of the goldfish bags. Water began to squirt out and the goldfish

33

was left flopping in an almost empty bag. The guy grabbed the bag and put the fish in a new bag of water. We laughed so hard our stomachs were hurting. The goldfish guy didn't seem too happy. We decided we'd better try a different game, something with no sharp, pointy objects.

Before long, we saw Daddy and Mama. Catherine was pretty tired of walking with her heavy cast. She held onto my shoulder as we walked back towards the truck. Mark and James came running towards us just as we reached the exit gate.

"Hey girls!" They yelled.

"Did you guys enjoy the fair?" I asked.

They looked at each other and laughed.

"Uh, yeah, we've just been walking around," James responded. "Our dad is waiting for us in the car. He's going to drop us off at home when we leave from here."

"My mom will be coming to pick me up tonight," Catherine said with raised eyebrows and a smile.

"Maybe James and I can come over when we get home," Mark said happily.

Catherine couldn't stop grinning. I knew that was exactly what she wanted them to say. Truthfully, I did, too.

"I'm sure Mama and Daddy won't mind," I remarked.

James and Mark walked us to the truck. Before we could say anything, Mama invited the boys over for ice cream and cookies.

"Your mom is so nice," Catherine whispered.

She and I climbed into the truck. We talked and laughed all the way home.

It didn't take Mama long to scoop up the ice cream. James and Mark came over as soon as their dad dropped them off. They were pretty tired, so they said they were not going to stay very long. Mama put the cookie jar on the table. We ate until all of the cookies were gone.

"So, what did you guys do at your dad's?" I asked.

"We helped Dad at his training center," Mark said.

Catherine and I were curious about this training center.

"What kind of training?" Catherine asked.

"Oh, gymnastics and stunts," James responded.

"That sounds exciting," I exclaimed.

"It's hard work," Mark said, yawning.

"Did you guys like the stilt-walkers in the parade?" I asked with excitement.

"Uh, yeah, we did," James said.

"I got a lot of the candy they were throwing. I even have some left," I said, as I took everything out of my pocket to show them.

"Hey," James cried. "Why do you have Catherine's rock?"

"I was just holding it for her because she didn't have a pocket," I responded. "Anyway, how did you know it was Catherine's?"

"Uh, ESP, I guess. You know, extra sensory perception," James quickly said.

I handed the rock to Catherine.

"I wonder what the W stands for?" Catherine asked.

"Maybe it's for the stilt-walker's name," I suggested. "One thing's for sure, we'll never know."

"Well, maybe they'll come back to town soon. Then you'll have a chance to ask them. I want to know, too," said James.

"Me too," Mark said, as he yawned again.

Catherine's mother came to pick her up. This time we waved and said bye. Mark and James got ready to leave, too.

"Do you think you'll come tomorrow to help sell ice cream?" I asked Mark.

"I have to help my grandmother tomorrow, but maybe James can come in my place," Mark said.

James smiled and nodded his head. Then they walked across the grass to their back yard. Mark turned and looked back. He waved as they went through the gate.

Mark is pretty nice, I thought. And so is James.

I went inside to a quiet house.

CHAPTER 6

Rise and Shine

The Sugar Shack was almost completely repaired. Daddy had worked very hard to finish it. James came over to help sell ice cream, like Mark had suggested. On his way over, he stopped by the Sugar Shack and talked with Daddy. I had been up for a while, just thinking and looking out of my window at the birds as they fluttered and splashed in the small birdbath in the middle of Mama's flower garden.

Daddy always said, "Early to bed and early to rise, makes a man healthy, wealthy and wise."

I guess that works for a young lady, too.

I couldn't believe how fast I got dressed. I wanted to hear what James and Daddy were talking about. James was just a few months older than me. They probably were talking 'man talk', sports, politics or cars. Anyway, I was curious.

Trying to look older, I cuffed my jeans up to the middle of my calves and unbuttoned the top button on my sleeveless, white blouse. My rolled down socks and white tennis shoes highlighted my ankle bracelet. I had already brushed my hair into a ponytail. As I checked myself one last time in the mirror, I realized that I was making more of a fuss about James than I did for Mark. I ran outside to the driveway by the Sugar Shack.

"Good Morning, Gwen. Come on over," Daddy said.

I was careful not to get grass stains on my shoes.

"Hi James," I smiled. "You're an early riser too, huh?"

"Yeah, every morning Grandma says, "Rise and shine boys. Time to get up and work. She says that even if we have nothing to do."

We all laughed. Daddy said, "There's nothing wrong with rising and shining. Like the old song says, "Rise, Shine, Give God the Glory."

James looked down at the ground. I could tell he was uncomfortable talking 'church talk'. James stopped coming to church last year when he and Mark's parents got a divorce. Their mother became an airline stewardess and was gone most of the time and their father moved to the other side of town. James and Mark didn't want to change schools, so they stayed with their grandmother.

James and I went to the porch to set up for the day. People seemed to be coming for Mama's ice cream a little slowly. Probably because the fair was in town.

"Hey!" I shouted, "How about we set up a booth and sell ice cream at the fair!"

"That's a great idea," Mama agreed. "I'll call Mr. Franklin at the City Commissioner's office right away. There shouldn't be a problem getting permission to sell at the fair because Mr. Franklin buys my ice cream all the time."

James was happy to go with us to the fairgrounds the next day. He even seemed excited to sell Mama's ice cream. Mama said she would pay him $10.00 to help her at the fair.

"I'll come for the rest of the week. My grandma won't mind." James said.

Mama smiled. I think she really likes James. I was beginning to like him, too. Mr. Franklin met us at the fairground entrance and showed us where to set up. Daddy unloaded the truck and went back home to finish working on the Sugar Shack. Mama, James and I arranged everything inside the little, wooden booth. Mama asked James if he would crank the handle on the ice cream freezer. With no refrigerator nearby, the ice cream was melting pretty fast. Mama had to keep it in the metal container in the ice cream freezer. I kept putting ice and rock salt around the container as James cranked the handle to keep the cream frozen. Rock salt keeps the ice from melting so fast.

In the center of the fairgrounds, people began to gather around the big, wooden stage.

"Dance Contest," the announcer said. "Sign up here to participate."

"We should sign up," James said. "Can you dance?"

Mama butted in, laughing, "Gwen can cut a rug."

"That means I can really dance," I told James, as I jokingly patted myself on the back.

"Can you dance?" I asked.

"I try," James grinned.

Mama said she could manage the ice cream booth alone for a little while.

We quickly signed up. Every dance team was given a number, and we were number six. The music started and the first contestants danced. Everyone who had gathered around the stage to watch, applauded for each participant. When it was our turn, James took my hand and spun me around. We moved to the beat and shook our hips. James even did a flip and danced impressively like the stilt-walkers. The next performers were a sister and brother team who did acrobatic stunts between their dancing. James and I thought that they would probably win. When the announcer excitingly said that we were the winners, James and I jumped up and hugged each other. His cologne smelled so nice and I liked the feel of his strong arms. We ran back to the ice cream booth with our first place trophies. Mama was very happy for us.

I looked forward to going to the fair every day. James and I were becoming close friends. Each day Mama's sales doubled. We all were very impressed. By the end of the week, Mama had made ten times more money than she had made selling from the porch. She paid James his ten dollars and she even gave me ten dollars. Daddy was able to finish the Sugar Shack, pay off the bills and even put some money in savings for me to go to college. He had added a little patio onto the back of the shack and he even added a small wooden picnic table with a bench big enough for two people to sit. James and I decided to try it out.

"So, what are you going to do with your ten dollars, Gwen?" James asked.

"I'm going to buy some material for Mama to make me a new yellow dress," I said proudly. "What are you going to do with yours?"

"I'm going to give half of it to Mark because he did my chores for me this week, so I could work for your mom," James said.

"That's really nice of you," I complimented.

I felt pretty selfish. James hadn't been to church in over a year and look how thoughtful he was. I went every Sunday and I only thought about myself. I wonder what James would be like if he went to church every week?

"You ever think about coming back to church, James?" I asked.

James began to share what happened to his family last year.

"Early one Friday morning," James said sadly, "Mom took Mark and me to school. We were having a special band rehearsal that day. Mom was dressed as though she was on her way to work. Dad always left for work every morning at six o'clock. When he got to work, he was feeling pretty sick so his boss sent him home for the day. On his way home, as he drove past the church, he saw Mom's car parked next to Deacon Stockwell's car in the parking lot. Deacon Stockwell had a cleaning business and was responsible for cleaning the church."

"I remember," I interrupted. "His wife died several years ago. She was a hair stylist at her own beauty shop while Deacon Stockwell ran the cleaning business."

"Yeah, well," James said, "Dad walked in and found him and Mom hugged up together, laughing and talking. He was so angry, he punched Deacon Stockwell in the face, who later found out that his nose was broken. The Pastor called them all in for a counseling session. The only thing that came out of that was that Mom and Dad were going to get a divorce. Dad told us some of what happened, but he never told us any details. Many, many times, I overheard several of the church members talking about the incident. Some even turned up their noses at us when we walked in with Dad. Dad didn't complain when I told him I didn't want to go to church anymore."

As James talked, I thought, It's nice to be the listening ear for someone who needs to just talk.

James sat pulling the string from the raveled edge of his cut-off jeans.

"That's sad, James," I finally said.

"The sad part about it all is that nobody helped Mark and me. Nobody seemed to care about us at all," James said, "Not even the youth leaders."

"My family and I care about you," I sympathetically said.

"I thought you cared about Mark," James said.

"No," I smiled, "I think Mark and Catherine care about each other."

"I don't know," James replied. "Mark keeps telling me about a guy named Wesley at the church. He and Catherine were good friends before she and her family moved."

"WESLEY!" I yelled. "That could be what the 'W' on the rock stands for."

"Maybe the stilt-walker was Wesley," James said.

Wesley had never said anything about it at church.

"Well," James said, "Enough about them. I guess I'd better be getting home. I'm going to miss going to work at the fair."

James took my hand, "I'm going to miss you, too," he smiled.

"Maybe you can go to church with me tomorrow. Many of the old members have left and the new members don't know about the past," I suggested.

"Thank you for your caring, listening ear, Gwen. I think I'll give church a try again," James said.

"You can ride with us," I grinned. "But one thing is for sure, you have to rise and shine early like your grandma says."

"Now, that, I can do," laughed James. "I'll see you bright and early tomorrow."

James walked away smiling. I was smiling, too.

CHAPTER 7

Just Tell The Whole Truth

I couldn't believe how fast James got back into the swing of things at church. One thing I learned about James is that he is not shy at all. Miss Myrtle talked him into joining the church Theatrics Ministry. Every Thursday night they have practice. Miss Myrtle used to perform at the local theater, so she knew a lot about Performing Arts. She said that James had great potential as an actor, so she didn't hesitate to give him a major part in the upcoming play. He's supposed to be a cripple, old man who wants to be the director of the church choir. James practices so much until sometimes his cripple walk seems real.

Most of the people at church seem to really like James, especially the youth in the Youth Fellowship. They think James is so funny. At the last youth meeting, I announced that I was having a birthday party and I gave invitations to all 25 members. I wanted this to be a very special party since I was turning 16. Jan Rayburn asked if James was going to be the entertainment. She knew that James and I were pretty close friends. I smiled at James.

"I just might do that," James said.

"Where is Mark?" I asked.

"He's been spending most of his free time talking on the phone with Catherine," James said. "I think he's making sure she's not interested in Wesley."

Now that James and I are together, I think Catherine and Mark make a cute couple, even though they are just 15. Mama and Daddy said it's okay for me to have James as a friend as long as we are not serious at this age.

On the evening before my birthday, Daddy, James and I decorated for my party. Daddy put up an aluminum awning covering from the side of the Sugar Shack roof. He called it a car port. I called it a patio. Well, whatever it's called, that's where my party was going to be. I had already called and invited Catherine, but she couldn't come to spend the night and help decorate. That's why James came to help. Mama was doing all of the cooking (fried chicken, potato salad, cake and ice cream). The first batch of candy Mama made in the newly repaired Sugar Shack was especially for my birthday celebration. I couldn't help but feel so special and so loved. James and Daddy hung a long string of lantern-shaped, patio lights around the edge of the awning. Benches, tables and lawn chairs created a border for the party area. Daddy made a small platform for the DJ, Karaoke machine and microphone.

"Well, Gwen, what do you think?" Daddy asked.

"I love it Daddy. You really know how to set up for a party," I said.

"I've thrown some pretty good parties in my day," Daddy proudly said.

Mama grinned and nodded her head. They walked hand-in-hand back up to the house. James and I sat outside the Sugar Shack admiring the bright moon and the twinkling stars in the night sky.

"I hope my party will be fun," I said. "It surely would be great if I could have the stilt-walkers here. Then my party would be super great!" I exclaimed.

"You really liked those stilt-walkers, huh?" James said. "Well, your party is going to be super anyway because you are a super person."

"Hey!" James shouted, "I still have to get you a gift! What would you like?"

"Oh, you've done enough for me already," I smiled. "Just being here with me at my party will be enough."

I felt good saying that. It reminded me of how I'm supposed to think of others more than myself. That's what our Pastor always says.

James stood up and stretched, as if he were measuring the height of the awning.

"I guess I'd better be going," he said. "Got to get my clothes ready for the party. Mark and I will be here early."

"See you tomorrow," I said.

When the sun rose the next morning and the dew dried on the grass, I ran outside to make sure everything was still in place for the party. I wiped off the chairs and covered the tables with Mama's red and white tablecloths. Catherine and her mother drove up just as I finished. They marveled at how pretty everything looked as we walked back to the house. Catherine and I spent hours in my room trying new hair styles and getting dressed for my party. I felt so 'grown up' in my new jeans and my short-sleeved, pink blouse, with my hair pulled up in a bun.

Mama had asked Catherine's mother to help her with the food, so they spent most of the day in the Sugar Shack. Mrs. Armstead was good company for Mama while Daddy made sure the yard looked nice around the shack. James and Mark came at about 4:00. They both had on jeans and t-shirts. I thought they would be dressed in some nice slacks and classy shirts. Catherine and I looked at each other. I could tell she was thinking the same thing I was thinking, but we didn't say anything that might make James and Mark feel bad.

Jan Rayburn and her brother Cory came right at 5:00 when the party was actually supposed to start. Cory was 18 and was the DJ for just about every local party. It didn't take him long to set up and start the music. Most of the party guests arrived shortly after Cory had finished setting up. He knew exactly what to play to get the people up and dancing. Line dancing was very popular because no one had to have a partner. We did every line dance we could think of, and we even made up our own steps to create a new line dance.

Just as Cory announced that it was karaoke time, a black van pulled into the driveway. I was surprised when James and Mark's dad got out. He was not there long before James said they had to leave for a while. He said they had to do some work for their dad. I couldn't believe that their dad would make them leave in the middle of the party. They climbed into the back of the van. The windows were tinted so I couldn't even see them to know whether they were waving or not. Catherine and I sat on the bench staring as the van slowly backed out of the driveway and drove away.

"Well, what was that all about?" Catherine asked.

"Maybe they don't like us anymore," I suggested.

"Well, it would be nice if they would just tell us and stop keeping secrets," Catherine said.

Cory invited people to sign up to sing. Myrtle Sinclair and her brother Joe sang first. They sang 'Moon River'. I closed my eyes and pictured James and me waltzing around a big ballroom. For a moment I was sad because James was not here, but I remembered I had to make sure everyone was having a good time, since it was my party.

I spotted Marion Cassidy sitting in the corner thumbing through Cory's list of songs.

Oh no, I thought, Marion has a voice that sounds like a frog. What in the world is she going to sing?

She picked up the microphone and began to sing Amazing Grace. I clapped after she sang the first verse, hoping that would make her stop. It only made her sing louder. I didn't want anyone to laugh or make fun of her, so I joined in and sang with her. When we finished, Mama said the food was ready.

Perfect timing, I thought.

Everyone cheered and clapped. You couldn't tell if they were clapping for our singing or because it was time to eat. Either way, Marion was happy. We all sat around eating and talking as Cory played more lively music. Before we were through eating, James came back dressed in black slacks and a nice, royal blue, short sleeve, silky shirt. He said Mark would be coming back soon. James had been rushing to get back to my party, so I made him a plate of food while he sat to catch his breath. Daddy turned the lantern lights on as the sun began to set. A large, brown van pulled into the driveway. I thought someone was being picked up from the party early. The driver was dressed in red, green and black. He got out and opened the back of the van. To our surprise, out came three drummers and two stilt-walkers.

"Oh, I can't believe it!" I screamed.

The drummers played and the stilt-walkers danced just like they did in the parade. Daddy, Mama and Mrs. Armstead came out of the Sugar Shack.

"Thank you Mama and Daddy!" I shouted, jumping up and down.

"Don't thank us," Daddy said. "This is just as much of a surprise to us as it is to you."

James is the only one who knew I wanted to have the stilt-walkers here," I told Mama and Daddy. "Maybe he got them for me!"

"I'm sure this group costs too much for James to pay," Daddy said.

I whispered to James, "Did you pay for these stilt-walkers?"

"No!" he replied. "I don't have that kind of money."

"Well," I exclaimed, "I don't know who to thank."

Marion chimed in, "Just say thank you Jesus."

"She's right," Mama agreed.

I turned to watch the performers. They danced around in a circle and motioned for everyone to dance with them. We had to be careful not to knock them down. Everyone danced except Marion.

It amazes me how some people can try to be so holy that they can't even have fun.

"Come on Marion," Wesley said.

But Marion just stood there watching.

After about twenty minutes, the drummers got back into the van. One of the stilt-walkers took a small, white box out of his shirt pocket and gave it to me. Written on the outside of the box in small letters were the words "Happy Birthday, Gwen!"

I held the box tightly in my hand as I watched the tall stilt-walkers walk gracefully to the van. They both slid into the back and the driver closed the doors. We all waved and watched as he drove slowly down the unpaved road.

"Well," I told James, "I guess that W doesn't stand for Wesley. He's here at the party."

Marion said the stilt-walkers at my party must have been a miracle. Mark came back about an hour after the stilt-walkers left. He was wearing black pants and a blue shirt and tie. He smelled like freshly sprayed cologne.

"You look nice Mark," Catherine smiled.

Mark smiled with his chin up and his chest out. "All for you, My Dear."

"You missed the stilt-walkers," I whined. "They were here at my party. Even the drummers came and played while the stilt-walkers danced for about twenty minutes. And look what they gave me!"

I held out the little, white box. James opened it for me. Inside was a beautiful, gold bracelet with a heart charm hanging down. He fastened it on my wrist.

"I think that stilt-walker likes you," James said.

Then he hugged me and whispered, "So do I."

On Sunday, at church, my friends told me how good my party was. Even Marion said she had a fun time. She even thanked me for singing with her. James and Mark didn't come to the morning service. They were going to wait and come to the evening service. They had already asked Daddy if they could get a ride with us.

When we pulled into the driveway after church, I glanced at the Sugar Shack. I could still visualize the stilt-walkers dancing in our yard.

What a miracle, I thought.

Once inside the house, I went straight to my room. After laying my 'Sunday dress' across the foot of my bed, I curled up under my long, soft throw blanket and went to sleep.

Taking a nap in the middle of the day sure did feel good. By the time I awakened, ate a little food, freshened myself up and put my dress back on, it was time to go back to church. Daddy stopped to pick up James and Mark, who were standing on their front porch waiting.

"How's your grandmother?" I asked as they climbed into the car.

"She's doing fine," Mark said. "Catherine calls her almost every other day. She likes talking to Grandma about becoming a nurse."

James sat next to me. He looked at my gold bracelet and smiled. When we got to church, we sat in the front with the rest of the youth.

Pastor Craig opened the evening service by inviting anyone to come up and testify. He said God is no respecter of persons, so anyone can testify, even young people. Marion quickly tapped me on the shoulder.

"You should tell about the stilt-walker miracle," she convincingly said.

I walked up to the front and took the microphone. I began telling how God sent the stilt-walkers to my party. I told how it was a real miracle because no one knew I wanted the stilt-walkers to come, nor could anyone afford to pay for them to perform.

Everyone began clapping and praising God. Eight year old, Melissa, even wanted to touch my hand in hopes that some of the blessing would rub off on her.

I was feeling pretty special when I sat back down in my seat.

Pastor Craig's sermon was about truth and lies. He said that one lie leads to another lie. And even if the truth hurts, it will eventually set you free. So it's best to just tell the whole truth.

James kept squirming in his seat like a little kid. By the end of the sermon, his face was as pale as a bleached pair of jeans and his eyes were pink, as if he had a cold.

When Pastor Craig got ready to close out the service, he said, "All minds clear?"

James raised his hand and stood up.

He said, "Pastor, I need to tell the whole truth."

Everyone looked at him. Those who knew what happened to his parents gasped as if they thought he was going to tell about what happened.

Pastor gave him the microphone. James began to talk in a soft, wobbly voice. It sounded like he was about to cry. Mark went up and stood next to him.

James said, "Mark and I have a job. We've been working for my dad. We entertain for special events, parties and even parades. Our identity while performing is supposed to be kept a secret to create a mystifying uniqueness, but it has created an untruth, and the lives of others are affected."

James continued to talk, "The truth is, my brother and I are the stilt-walkers. I wanted to do something special for my friend's birthday party, so I told one lie, then another, and another. I didn't know it would create all of this talk about a miracle. I'm sorry everyone."

Tears rolled down my cheeks as James and Mark walked down the aisle and out of the church. I don't know if I was crying because I was sad for James or if I was sad that it was not a miracle. Anyway, James didn't even look at me and now they were nowhere to be found.

Daddy and Mama felt responsible for them, since their grandmother expected us to bring them home.

We got in the car as quickly as we could. As Daddy drove, Mama and I looked on both sides of the street. About two blocks from the church, sitting at the bus stop, we spotted them. Daddy pulled over and smiled.

Mama said, "We surely do need some help eating the left over ice cream from the party. We would love to give you a ride. I don't think your grandmother will mind you stopping by for a little while."

James looked at me with droopy, sad eyes. I could tell he was so embarrassed so I smiled and motioned for them to get in. He and Mark were so quiet on the way home. I didn't say anything either because I didn't want to say the wrong thing.

Mama, James, Mark and I got out and went in the Sugar Shack while Daddy parked the car. Mark called their grandmother to let her know where they were. Their grandmother is as trusting of them as Mama and Daddy are of me.

Mama gave each of us a big bowl of peach ice cream topped with whipped cream and a cherry. She and Daddy said good night and went up to the house.

I cleared my throat and gathered enough courage to say, "That was a brave thing you did at church tonight, James."

"I felt so badly about the miracle thing," James said. "I just couldn't let it continue."

"How are there always two stilt-walkers?" I asked James, puzzled.

"Sometimes Mark and my dad perform, and sometimes it's my dad and me. We take turns to keep people who know us from suspecting that it's us."

James took my arm and opened the little heart that dangled from the bracelet. Inside were the letters J/G.

"They stand for James and Gwen," He said.

I had not noticed that the heart could even open.

"The nicest thing about all of this is not so much about hearing the truth, but knowing that this bracelet is from you," I smiled.

I was suddenly so in love. And at that moment, nothing else was important.

CHAPTER 8

What Matters

The day of the church play was rapidly approaching. I couldn't wait to see how James' part fit in the plot of the story. James said that every time he practiced his part, he got sad because of how his character was supposed to be treated in the story.

"When you have a physical problem," he said, "It's sad that people treat you like you have no feelings."

"But, this is just a play," I reminded him.

"I know, but it's reality," James responded. "People treat you like you don't even matter."

"Make up some new lines," I suggested. "Tell about your feelings. Tell what it's really like, from the cripple man's point of view."

"I asked Miss Myrtle if I could, and she said no. It's her way or no way."

On the night of the play, the audience was packed. James' dad and grandmother sat on the front row. Mark, Catherine and I sat on the second row behind them. Mama was in the choir and Daddy had to usher.

Just before the play started, Mrs. Bell came in, pushing Aunt Wanda in a wheelchair. She rolled her right next to the front row which was near the stage. Aunt Wanda had been having trouble walking since the day she fell going down Mrs. Bell's front porch steps. I was surprised to see either of them. Mrs. Bell had told Mama how hard it was to take care of Ms. Wanda since she couldn't walk very well. Aunt Wanda spotted Mama in the choir. She frantically waved at Mama as if she was so happy to see her. Mrs. Bell could have sat on the front row next to Aunt Wanda, but she found a seat three rows behind her. Aunt Wanda couldn't even see her.

Finally, the lights were dimmed and the play started. The choir followed the script as the tenors sang the wrong notes and some of the sopranos tried to sing louder than everyone else. They were obviously not organized because they didn't have a director. Throughout the play, different people tried out for the choir director's position. Some were qualified and some were not. But, what the leaders in the church wanted was someone who was well known and popular in the city. They felt that a popular person would make the choir and the church look good.

When it was James' turn to try out, he entered the stage walking cripple like he was supposed to, and according to the script, nobody knew him. Some of the choir members laughed. People in the audience began to laugh, too. I could tell that James was very sad.

He introduced himself to the choir, "I'm Henry Cook. I can play the piano, organ, drums and bass guitar. I sing and I can teach songs with four part harmony."

Rudely, someone in the choir yelled, "You can do all of that with your infirmity?"

A few of the choir members laughed. Some even turned up their noses and walked out. Some decided to take a short break until Henry's turn was up. Some felt sorry for him and brought him a chair.

Why would Miss Myrtle write a script like that? I wondered.

James couldn't take it anymore, so he decided to change his script.

He took the microphone and told the choir, "I know I'm not famous, nor am I handsome to look at because of my handicap. But, if you can follow my directing, together we can create a sound that will be pleasing to God, because that's what matters, if it is pleasing to God."

The other choir members returned. They looked confused. They all knew that James was not following the script. No one said anything. James directed Mrs. Jones to play the introduction to the song. He raised his arms and began to direct. The choir followed with a new seriousness, as if they were singing for real and not just part of a play. The song was exceptionally beautiful. Everyone clapped. The curtains closed and Miss Myrtle said we would have a fifteen minute intermission. I swallowed hard for fear that she would be upset with James for changing the script. Sure enough, she was very upset. She yelled at James like he was two years old. The other cast members stood around and watched. Miss Myrtle said she didn't know how to fix the play now.

"The rest of the script won't fit," she cried.

She accused James of sabotaging the play, after all of her hard work. She looked at the cast and nodded as if she was trying to get everyone to agree with her. James came out and leaned against the wall near the front row. Aunt Wanda could tell that something was wrong. She began to unlock her chair.

She motioned for James to come and help her. After James told her what happened, she told him to push her up to the stage behind the curtain. James thought she wanted to talk to Miss Myrtle, but she didn't. She wanted the microphone. Anyway, Miss Myrtle had gone home with a bad headache.

James gave Aunt Wanda the microphone and slowly opened the curtains. Aunt Wanda began to talk as if she was a part of the play.

"I'm the Mother of this church," she said. "And I have never heard this choir sing so well. I say we choose this young man for our new choir director."

The other cast members came and stood around James. Aunt Wanda led the group in what ended up being a unanimous vote. Henry would be the new director.

Aunt Wanda said, "From now on, we are going to be more compassionate to those with physical problems, and treat each other with respect. Now, LET THE CONCERT BEGIN!"

Having said that, James rolled Aunt Wanda next to the alto section in the choir. Mama wrote the names of five songs that she knew the choir could sing. She gave the list to James and Mrs. Jones. They nodded because they knew the songs, also. The choir sang, directed by Henry Cook. He even used his cripple walk while he directed. People said that was the best play they had seen in a long time. James thanked the cast for adjusting nicely to the new script.

I felt badly for Miss Myrtle. She didn't even know that the play was a big success. If she hadn't been so concerned about herself and her fame, she would have realized that what James said in the play was really worth saying.

The next day, the Pastor said he wanted to meet with James and Miss Myrtle after church. James was not very excited about that because he figured Miss Myrtle must have told Pastor Craig what he had done.

"I'll go with you, James, since I was the one who encouraged you to change the script," I said.

After church, Mama and Daddy waited for us in the car.

Pastor Craig told Miss Myrtle that he was so proud of her and the theatrics members for putting on such a wonderful play. He thanked her for her dedicated service to the ministry. We each had a turn to talk. No one yelled or treated anyone with disrespect. Miss Myrtle talked first and shared how difficult it is when the script is changed.

"It was my suggestion to change the script," I told Miss Myrtle. "I understand how you feel and I'm sorry. Please forgive me."

James explained how he felt about his character's treatment. And even though the play had to be altered, he didn't appreciate being yelled at like he was a nobody.

Miss Myrtle held her head down. She frowned as if she was in deep thought about what James had said.

Then, apologetically, she said, "I'm sorry, James, for yelling at you. Please forgive me."

Pastor Craig spoke last, "This was a good meeting. Sharing your feelings allows the others involved to understand the situation better. It's easier to apologize and ask for forgiveness that way."

Pastor Craig spoke with authority, "Even though mending earthly relationships is very important, asking God to forgive us is what really matters. It's up to each of you to ask for forgiveness for what you feel you did that was not pleasing to God."

We all prayed right then and there.

Daddy and Mama would have been proud of me...again.

CHAPTER 9

Silent Night

Catherine's cast would be coming off in one week. She wanted to spend the night before it was time to go back to school. Aunt Wanda returned to stay with us the night after her big debut in the play and she seemed so much happier.

Daddy made a wooden ramp on the side of the front porch so we could roll Aunt Wanda's wheelchair up and down easily. Mama's candy and ice cream sales were unbelievable. Big companies were ordering candy in bulk. We all had to help because Mama just couldn't make that much candy that fast. Mama hired James and Mark as employees. They took the orders and Daddy collected the money. Mama and I made the candy and ice cream. Of course, Daddy and James took turns cranking the handle on the ice cream freezer.

The Sugar Shack was always full of customers. Even though Aunt Wanda's singing brought more people, many days she didn't feel like singing like she had done on the porch. Plus, Mama couldn't handle too many more customers.

Mama and I had a routine for taking care of Aunt Wanda. One of us would push her in her wheelchair back up to the house and to her room. The other would help her prepare for bed. It became easier as time passed. Plus, Aunt Wanda had lost a lot of weight. Mama was a little concerned about that.

Usually, at the end of the day, when all of the customers were gone, the night would be so peaceful. Daddy and Mama were always so exhausted after cleaning and putting everything away. Every night, as soon as his job was finished, Mark would go home. He said his feet were always so tired.

"Come on, Sugar," Daddy said to Mama one night. "Time to go back up to the house."

I'd never heard Daddy call Mama 'Sugar' before.

"This is something new," I whispered to James.

Daddy took a little pink box out of the storage cabinet. He hid it behind his back so Mama wouldn't see it. Putting his finger over his lips, he motioned for James and me to be quiet.

"Good night," we said, as they closed the door to the shack.

James and I sat on the little patio for a while, just listening to the chirping of the crickets. He put his arm around my shoulders.

"Look at the night sky," he said. "God has placed his shining moon and twinkling stars in this huge sea of darkness. It's almost unbelievable that God is even mindful of us."

"That's because he loves us," I said.

James gently cupped his hands around my face. He slowly leaned in close and kissed me gently on my cheek. I melted into his arms, and we stayed there for a long time.

James held my hand as we finally walked up to the house. The front porch light was always on after dark. Two moths fluttered around the light as if they were dancing. James twirled me around and we waltzed across the front porch, mimicking the moths. I giggled quietly so I wouldn't wake up Aunt Wanda. Her room was closest to the front door.

"Aunt Wanda is still asleep," I whispered.

"Yeah," James said softly, "I can hear her snoring."

"She snores loud like that every night," I smirked.

"Well, guess we'd better get some sleep, too. Long day ahead of us tomorrow," James said softly.

He kissed the back of my hand and bowed like a gentleman in a movie.

I watched him jog across the yard to his house.

He seems as happy as I am, I thought with a smile.

I carefully opened the door, trying not to make any noise. The box that Daddy had hidden behind his back was sitting on the coffee table in the living room.

"Looks like Mama and Daddy had a little celebration while I was outside," I chuckled.

Two cards lay on the table next to a cute little blue and pink music box. Anniversary wishes were on each card. They reminded me of the time when Daddy kissed Mama on the cheek in front of me. Mama got so embarrassed, she almost dropped the dish of food she was carrying.

I remember Daddy laughing and saying, "Gwen, when you get married, always remember that it's important to keep every day exciting and new so your marriage won't get old and dull."

I tiptoed to my room thinking how lucky I was to have good role models like Mama and Daddy.

I opened my window just enough to feel the balmy, summer-night's breeze. Many thoughts filled my mind as I crawled into my bed. I couldn't go to sleep for thinking about how my life seemed to be changing. Love at 16 is hard to deal with. It makes you think more about your future.

Aunt Wanda used to always say, "Now, Child, you've got to always keep things in order, FIRST THINGS FIRST."

Then she would explain to me how you put the right sock on first, then the left, because the right is more important than the left.

When I laughed and asked her if that was really true, she smiled and said, "Yes, you know the Bible says Jesus sits on the right hand of the Father, so I figure right is more important."

I love Aunt Wanda. She says and does so many funny things. I think James loves her, too. He's just as caring with her as I am.

It took forever for me to fall asleep, but I finally did.

Catherine called early the next morning. She and her mother were on their way to our house. I rolled out of bed and slid slowly to the floor. Mama and Daddy were up already, as usual. Breakfast was cooked and warming in the oven. Mama was helping Aunt Wanda get cleaned up and dressed for the day.

"Good Morning," I said as I came out of my room.

Aunt Wanda smiled when she saw me.

"Looks like you could use a little more sleep," she said.

"I really could," I replied. "I didn't sleep well. I guess I was thinking too hard."

"I didn't sleep well either," Aunt Wanda yawned. "I kept dreaming about a lot of little children playing and laughing."

"I wonder what that was all about?" Mama said rather puzzled.

Then she quickly changed the subject, "Another long day ahead of us, Gwen."

I grabbed a couple of pieces of bacon and went to my room to get dressed. We all were down at the Sugar Shack at seven thirty. James and Mark arrived at about the same time. I parked Aunt Wanda's wheelchair next to the table in the back room and gave her a glass of water. She said she was all set for the day and didn't need anything else right then.

We were working very hard when Catherine and her mother drove up. Catherine's cast was off and she walked slinging her left leg out as if she wanted everyone to notice.

Mark began to laugh out loud, "Catherine, you're walking like a marionette puppet controlled by an amateur puppeteer."

"Hi, Mark, I'm happy to see you, too," Catherine said angrily. "And, why haven't you called me?"

"I've been working here at the Sugar Shack," he answered sharply.

"Sounds like you both got up on the wrong side of the bed this morning," James chimed in.

"They're just 15," I whispered to James when they weren't looking. "I guess they don't value their relationship like we do."

I felt pretty mature saying that. I gave Catherine a pat on the head. She walked into the back room and sat at the table with Aunt Wanda until Mama called her to help Mark take orders. I tried to brighten up the mood a little by asking Mama about her gift.

"Your daddy gave me a cute music box," Mama said with a big grin.

"What does it play?" I asked.

"It plays Silent Night," Mama proudly answered.

"That's my favorite song," Aunt Wanda said. "It doesn't matter if it's Christmas or not. I could listen to that song all day."

Aunt Wanda burst into a loud chuckle as if she had heard a funny joke.

"What's so funny, Mrs. Wanda?" Catherine yelled from the front counter.

"Oh, I was just thinking about the time my sister, God rest her soul, and I were decorating our Christmas tree. She wanted me to hang the ice cycles on the tree one by one like she was doing. But I wanted to just throw a hand full on the tree at one time. We started throwing icicles at each other. We had a time picking them all up from the floor."

Aunt Wanda looked sad, "Sure do miss my sister."

Just then the front door opened and in walked the first customer.

"Hi Catherine, fancy seeing you here," the customer said.

"Hi Wesley," Catherine smiled. "I like the painted rock you gave me."

Wesley looked surprised.

"What rock?" Mark asked defensively.

Catherine took the rock out of her pocket.

"This rock," Catherine said with a loving smile. "It has a 'W' on one side. I figured you knew the stilt-walker and told him to give it to me."

Mark grabbed the rock from Catherine's hand.

"I gave you this rock!" he yelled. "That's an M, not a W!"

Mark turned the rock right-side-up. Catherine was so embarrassed.

"I forgot to tell you," I quickly spoke. "Mark and James told us at church that they were the stilt-walkers."

"Why didn't you tell me, Mark?" Catherine cried.

"I guess I've been too busy," Mark said softly.

Wesley stood at the counter feeling very flattered.

"I'm not very busy this summer," he said with a sarcastic grin.

Mark grabbed Wesley by the collar.

"Mark!" I yelled, "You're a Junior Deacon. Don't mess up your reputation!"

Mark pushed Wesley away. Wesley ran out of the shack without buying one thing. Aunt Wanda began to sing,... Sleep in heavenly peace.

"Nothing like heavenly peace," she muttered.

James whispered something to Mark, and we all got back to work.

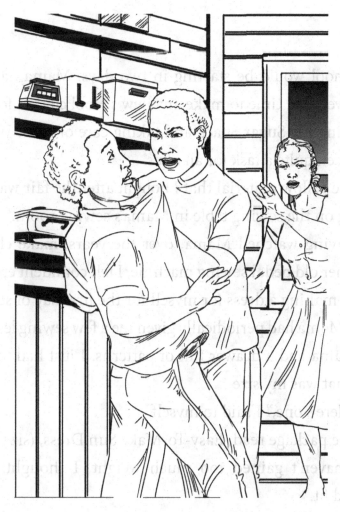

CHAPTER 10

YELLOW BUTTERFLY

School would be starting in two days. Mama had not even had time to make any new school clothes for me. Running the Sugar Shack and taking care of Aunt Wanda had been quite a task for all of us.

The yellow material that I bought after the fair was still laying on the sewing table in Mama's sewing room.

Having watched Mama, over the years, make clothes with her old pedal sewing machine, I felt confident enough to try making a dress for myself for the first day of school. Plus, Mama had periodically given me a few sewing lessons.

Mama had a drawer full of patterns. I just had to pick one that was my size.

"Here's one," I said to myself.

The package read, Easy-To-Make Sun Dress, (size 5).

I haven't gained too much weight, I thought. This should fit.

I pinned the pattern pieces on the material and began to cut. It wasn't long before I was ready to sew. Mama checked to make sure the machine was threaded correctly. I sewed and pressed each seam with the iron so the dress would be very neat, as I had seen Mama do. I sewed late into the night. The next morning, Mama saw my finished dress hanging by the sewing room.

"Couldn't have done a better job myself," Mama grinned. "Does it fit?"

"I hope so," I said. "I was too tired to try it on."

Mama's mouth fell open, "You must always take time to try it on before you finish it completely, in case you have to take something apart."

I took it into my room and put it on. When I came out, Mama had rolled Aunt Wanda out of her room to see it, too. They clapped when I came strutting down the hallway like a model.

"Perfect, Gwen," Mama said, pleasingly.

"You can make me one next," Aunt Wanda said. "Just measure me from hip to hip."

We all laughed. I'm sure she was just kidding.

On the way to church, we talked and laughed about what I could make and sell in the Sugar Shack.

"Since sewing has nothing to do with sugar," I joyfully said, "Mama, We'll have to change the name to Sugar's Shack. That's what Daddy called you on your Anniversary."

Mama blushed, as usual, and we went inside the church.

Pastor Craig prayed for all of the students. He always does that just before the first day of school. Wesley stood as far away from Mark as he could. He was still shaken up from the incident at the Sugar Shack. He had not been to any of the youth meetings and this was the first time I had seen him at church since that day. I saw Mark turn around. He spotted Wesley and began to move back to where Wesley was standing. Wesley's eyes got so big, I thought they were going to pop right out of his head. Mark put his hand on Wesley's shoulder. Then I saw the two of them shaking hands, and I knew they had made up.

Mark said that James told him he needed to make amends with Wesley before school resumed. He and Wesley would be attending the same high school. James had told him that high school is hard enough without having added stress from messed up friendships.

As we left church, Mark said that James should be the Junior Deacon. James put his arm across Mark's shoulder and gave him a 'knucklehead' rub. I waved as Mark and James got into Deacon Smith's car.

"See you later!" James yelled from the car.

When we got home, Aunt Wanda and I sat on the front porch while Mama fixed dinner. Daddy opened the Sugar Shack for a short time. He said the best time for a scoop of delicious ice cream is on a Sunday afternoon. He was so right.

Aunt Wanda's doctor had given her some new medicine that seemed to make her sleepy. Sometimes, when she would wake up from a short nap, she wouldn't know where she was. Sometimes she wouldn't even know who I was. She called me Gracie.

"It's me, Aunt Wanda, Gwen. I don't know anyone named Gracie," I would say.

Aunt Wanda would always smile and say, "Oh, yeah."

It was a beautiful day for sitting on the porch. We could hear the birds chirping in the trees. A butterfly fluttered across the porch.

"Oh, look Aunt Wanda, a yellow butterfly!" I shouted.

The same butterfly fluttered by three times, right in front of us. Seemed like it was putting on a show just for Aunt Wanda and me. We clapped, and the butterfly flew right over my head, then disappeared into the flowers.

That was amazing! We had seen many orange Monarch butterflies, but not a big yellow butterfly. Suddenly, I felt very sad. I didn't know why. Butterflies are so beautiful.

Did I really see that butterfly, or is that something that only happens in a daydream, I pondered.

I rolled Aunt Wanda inside. Daddy closed the Shack for the day. We all sat down and enjoyed a quiet Sunday dinner.

Bright and early Monday morning, I got dressed for school. Aunt Wanda was still asleep, and I could hear her snoring loudly. Mama said I looked cute in my yellow dress, white sandals and gold necklace with matching hoop earrings. Of course, I had on the gold bracelet that James gave me.

I walked to the bus stop with James and Mark. They had on nice slacks, new tennis shoes and button-down shirts with the sleeves rolled up. Their hair was cut and edged like a perfectly manicured lawn. Everyone at the bus stop told us how nice we looked. Sarah Giddens liked my dress. When I told her I made it, she asked if I could make her one. I told her that she could give me the material and I would make one for a small fee. She was serious and very pleased.

"I'll give it to you tomorrow," she said enthusiastically.

"Me too," said Clara Simpson.

"Well, I guess this is the start of my own business," I told James.

He smiled and said, "You can do it!"

He's so encouraging.

At school, James and I only had one class together. Mark said he had three classes with Wesley. James and I made a vow that we would graduate with honors as Valedictorians. All of our classes were college prep classes. An 'A' in those classes equaled two A's.

James had to stay for football practice after school, so Mark and I rode home on the bus together. I wanted to start reading some of my homework assignment, but Mark kept talking about the different kinds of rocks he had collected. He is very knowledgeable about rocks, but I surely wanted to throw one at him so he would be quiet.

When the bus stopped, Mark and I got off.

"Bye, Mark," I said gladly.

"See you tomorrow!" he yelled as he walked towards his house.

"Hey Everybody!" I called as I approached the Sugar Shack.

Mama and Daddy were making ice cream. No one was at the counter.

"Business was rather slow today," Daddy said.

"Where's Aunt Wanda?" I asked, looking in the back room.

"She didn't feel well, so I took her to her room to lay down and rest for a while," Mama replied. "The nurse came to see her today and she had a lot of papers for Wanda to sign in case something should happen to her."

"I'm going up to do my homework," I said. "I'll peek in and check on her."

Daddy said he would walk with me so he could tell me about Aunt Wanda's wishes.

As we approached Aunt Wanda's door, we could hear her snoring. I opened the door and Daddy and I tiptoed close to the bed.

"Oh, look Daddy," I whispered as I pointed to the window. "There's a yellow butterfly like the one Aunt Wanda and I saw the other day."

It was fluttering near the window as if it wanted to come in.

"Isn't that strange," I frowned. "Do you see it, Daddy?"

"Sure, I see it. It is unusual. I've never seen a big, yellow butterfly in this neck of the woods," Daddy replied.

This time, seeing the butterfly made me feel peaceful and calm. I pulled the cover up on Aunt Wanda's shoulders and Daddy and I went out.

"Mrs. Wanda is resting nicely," Daddy said.

He got Mama's red sweater and went back to the shack. I went into my room and closed the door. I could still hear Aunt Wanda snoring, but it was not disturbingly loud. I read page after page in my Literature book, analyzing important parts of the story. I had to write a paragraph on my thoughts and feelings about the main character. Then, I had to decorate the cover on the journal booklet we were given in class. I colored a blue sky, green grass with lots of colorful flowers, a window and a yellow butterfly.

Aunt Wanda woke up just in time for dinner.

"Getting a little cloudy outside," Daddy said. "Looks like we're going to get a little rain."

Mama gave Aunt Wanda her dinner in bed. She thanked Mama for all of her help. After dinner, I sat with Aunt Wanda for a while. I told her about my first day back at school. Some of my teachers, I told her, I liked. Others, I complained about.

As I talked, Aunt Wanda interrupted, "There is some good in the worst of us, and some bad in the best of us, so it little behooves any of us, to talk about the rest of us. Have you ever heard that saying?" Aunt Wanda asked me.

No," I answered. "But now I will always remember it."

Aunt Wanda looked tired. Mama came in to tuck her in for the night. Mama looked tired, too. Aunt Wanda wanted to hear Silent Night on Mama's music box. She loved that song. I wondered why she loved it so much. Maybe it was just because she missed her sister.

The next morning I got up earlier than usual.

"Jeans, white blouse, tennis shoes and ankle bracelet, sound good to wear to school today," I whispered to myself.

I looked out of my window. It had rained during the night. Beads of water decorated the grass and the flowers. I cracked my window to feel the cool breeze.

Aunt Wanda must be awake already, I thought, I don't hear her snoring.

I'll see if she needs anything before I leave for school. Seems like Mama could use a little more help.

I got dressed and walked out of my room. Aunt Wanda's door was open. Mama and Daddy were sitting on the side of her bed.

"She's gone," Mama whispered.

I looked at Aunt Wanda's peaceful face. Then I opened Mama's music box.

Pastor Craig pulled up in his car at the same time as the ambulance. There was no siren. All I could hear was the music from Mama's music box. Pastor Craig was not surprised to hear the Christmas song in September. He knew all about Mrs. Wanda's favorite song. He knew more than we knew because he knew Mrs. Wanda long before we met her.

James and Mark came running over when they saw the ambulance parked in our driveway.

"Aunt Wanda's gone," I sadly told them.

Daddy said I could stay home from school if I wanted to.

But I know what Aunt Wanda would have said, "Child, you better go on to school. First things first!"

James, Mark and I rode the bus to school. I could hear Silent Night ringing in my ears as I thought about Aunt Wanda. It was hard to concentrate in class, but I managed to stay focused.

The Sugar Shack was closed for the rest of the week. The funeral was on Saturday. No one had to do a lot of planning because Aunt Wanda had put everything in order before she got really sick.

At the funeral, I got up and talked. I told how Aunt Wanda was an amazing woman. I shared some of her funny sayings and I told how I had come to call her 'Aunt'. I shared my deepest feelings about my love for her. As I talked, a tall, slender lady began to cry. She had short, curly hair, a beautiful face and appeared to be in her late 60's. When I finished, she came to the microphone and hugged Pastor Craig as if she knew him.

Then she began to talk.

"My name is Grace. I am Mrs. Wanda's only daughter."

She began to weep bitterly as she told how she was a rebellious teenager and left home angry at age 16.

"The last Christmas that I spent at home," she said, "my mother gave me a beautiful, hand-carved, antique radio. Mother said it belonged to her mother. She turned it on and Silent Night was playing. She said, "Gracie, I don't understand your angry feelings towards me, but I'm giving this to you because you are my only child and I love you." I hugged my mother, which was something I hadn't done in several years. I took the radio and the next morning I left and never returned until today."

She told how Pastor Craig had left many messages before, but she had no desire, then, to see or talk to her mother.

As she walked back to her seat, between her sobs, she kept whispering, "Now I'm too late. I'm too late."

After the funeral, I wanted to talk to Grace, but I didn't know what to say. Really, I didn't know if I should be angry with her or sad for her.

I got into the car with Mama and Daddy. James and Mark rode home with their dad. I was alone in the back seat. No Aunt Wanda. No James. No Mark. No Catherine. I began to cry.

Mama said, "It's going to be alright, Gwen. The Lord said He would send a comforter."

Just then, the beautiful, yellow butterfly came fluttering directly at the windshield and flew up over the top of the car.

"Did you see that!" I squealed between sniffles.

I began to laugh. The more I laughed, the more my sadness disappeared.

"See, Gwen," Daddy said, "Everything is going to be alright."

CHAPTER 11

The Right Perspective
At The Right Time

Grace moved back to Warren shortly after Aunt Wanda's funeral. Mama hired her to work in the Sugar Shack since James, Mark and I were so busy. Every weekend I had a dress to make for somebody. With all of the leftover scraps of material, I made butterfly hair clamps. They were a big hit. I sold them for fifty cents. Some clamped on with a hairpin and some tied on with a thin ribbon.

James and I studied every evening on the patio in the back of the Sugar Shack. The desk from Aunt Wanda's room fit nicely in the corner of the patio. It was large enough for James and me to both study together. It was made of hard plastic. Aunt Wanda liked it because she could sit her glass of ice water on it and not warp the wood.

One evening while James and I were studying, Grace came out to get a breath of fresh air. She was wearing an apron that said New Orleans Mardi Gras Parade. James began to ask her about her apron. I couldn't believe he was showing her any interest after the way she had treated her mother. She could tell I didn't like her because I never looked up or joined in the conversation. In fact, I even rolled my eyes and smacked my lips when I heard her tell James about the stilt-walkers in the Mardi Gras parade. He told Grace about his father's training center and his stilt-walkers. Grace said she had connections in New Orleans and could get them a permanent place in the parade.

"The pay is real good," she said.

James packed up his books and said he had to go and tell his dad the news. I wanted to slap Grace, but I managed to maintain my composure long enough to pick up my books and go back to the house to study in my room. I threw my books on the bed, balled up my fist and gave my mattress a good sock. I don't know if I was more angry with Grace or James. I couldn't stay focused on my school work, so I decided to stop studying for the night.

The test we took the next day was very difficult. When the teacher returned our papers, I got a 'B'. James had an 'A'. I could kick myself. Why did I allow this situation to make me lose track of my future plans.

"I wish Grace would go back to where she came from," I angrily mumbled.

The next day, I just couldn't seem to get dressed fast enough. Daddy drove me to school because I missed the bus. James tried to talk to me at school and on the bus on the way home, but I pretended to be in a hurry and sleepy.

When we got off of the bus, he just went on home. Mama could tell something was wrong, but she didn't make a big deal about it. She knew I would eventually tell her.

"Mr. Mitchell was here to talk to Grace today," Mama calmly said.

"Yeah, James told her about his dad's business," I responded in a dull voice.

"I think they were making plans to go to the Mardi Gras," grinned Mama.

"That's big money for Mark and James," she continued.

I just couldn't make myself feel happy for them. I went to my room to rest.

On Friday, we took another test. I got a C+. James got an A.

When I got home, Daddy said, "The school counselor called today. He was concerned about your academic performance. Is there something you need to talk to us about, Gwen?"

Daddy always showed wisdom and integrity in every situation.

"No, Daddy," I replied. "I just have to get back on track."

"Remember, your mother and I are here if you need to talk," Daddy said, as he patted my shoulder.

"I know, Daddy. You and Mama are good parents," I said proudly.

I was up very early on Saturday morning. Mama and Daddy were still asleep. I went down to the Sugar Shack to work on the essay that was due on Monday.

I began to write:

Perspective is the outlook you have on things in life.

The way you see things can either be positive or negative, depending on whether you are optimistic or pessimistic. Your perspective is also based on your needs and what's important to you. That's why prioritizing life's necessities gives you a better opportunity to choose the right perspective at the right time...

Suddenly, I was interrupted

"Hello Gwen," the voice said.

Startled, I turned and looked. "Grace, what are you doing here so early?"

"Oh," she mumbled, "Just thought I'd get things started early so your mother won't have to work so hard today."

My heart began to pound. I could feel the blood rush to my face.

"Why are you being so nice to my mother when you couldn't even treat your own mother right?" I said angrily. "And why are you trying to take my friend and his family away?"

Grace sat in the chair across from me. I looked down at my paper to keep from looking at her. The first sentence of my essay stuck out as if someone was lifting it right off of the page. PERSPECTIVE IS...

I began to listen to Grace. She said that Aunt Wanda was really a good person and a good mother. She told me that she was so angry because her mother left her father when she was nine, and they moved to Arkansas.

Grace began to sniffle, "My mother tried to tell me how abusive my father was, but I didn't want to hear it."

"Perspective," I muttered.

"Yes," Grace said. "If I had the right perspective, I would have known that Mother was right for moving away and taking me with her. I'll never have the chance to tell my mother how wrong I was."

"So, you were angry with your mother for something she did to someone else," I smirked sarcastically.

"And you were angry with me for something I did to someone else," she smirked back.

I couldn't even deny that, so I said, "*There is some good in the worst of us...*"

Grace began to recite the same saying, "*And some bad in the best of us...*"

We laughed and gave each other a hug.

"Let's start all over," I said.

I reached out my hand, "Hi, I'm Gwendolyn Cole."

Grace shook my hand and said, "Nice to meet you. I'm Grace Tyler."

We sat down and continued our conversation. Only this time, we both talked with a new perspective. The right perspective.

"Where is your father?" I asked.

"I don't know," Grace replied. "We left him in New Orleans. That's why I've been living there, hoping to find him."

That night, I made a list of all of the things in life that were important to me; My parents, my education, a career, marriage, and friends. I figured God is naturally a part of everything, so I didn't write church on my list.

On Sunday, after church, I waited around for James to come out. I wanted to show him my list and share my feelings with my new outlook on life. When he finally came out, I didn't have a chance to say anything. He quickly gave me an envelope that said, *To Gwen.*

He licked his dry lips and said, "Read it when you get home."

Then he ran to his dad's van and they drove away.

I wasn't in a big hurry to read whatever was in that envelope, so I stuck it in my purse. I recall hearing people talk about a Dear John letter. I figured this might be one.

We enjoyed a peaceful afternoon together, just me, Mama and Daddy. They were at the top of my priority list, you know. Mama opened the Sugar Shack for a couple of hours to sell Sunday afternoon ice cream. Then she closed the Shack and we sat for a long time on the front porch.

"Sure do miss Aunt Wanda," I said. "Oh, by the way, Grace and I are friends now, and I have a new perspective on life."

Daddy chuckled, "Perspective, that's a good word."

"Yes," I smiled. "And I'm going to do better in everything."

Daddy and Mama were pleased to hear that. They knew I was serious because I went to my room to study a little more.

Late that night, I opened the envelope James had given me. Inside was a newspaper clipping. It read: NEW STILT-WALKER GROUP COMING TO NEW ORLEANS! There was a picture of two stilt-walkers, four drummers and Mr. Mitchell. Along with the article was a letter that James had written:

"Dear Gwen,"

I swallowed hard but I kept reading.

"My dad will be moving to New Orleans next year. My grandmother, Mark and I will be moving with him. Seems like life changes right before your eyes. Some things we have control over and some things we don't. I'll see you at school tomorrow. *Love James.*"

Next to his name he drew a heart with the letters J/G in the middle.

I took out my journal and wrote:

"In the quietness of this moment, I recognize and acknowledge that you are Almighty God. I thank you, Lord, for your Holy Spirit that helps me cling to the fruit that pleases you. You, I do love, because you ARE. Continue to help me listen as you tell me what to do. Good Night."

****

My senior year in high school was almost over. I could hardly believe it. James and his family had been gone since the end of my sophomore year. My future plans were falling in place nicely. I had already received a letter of acceptance to Spelman College in Atlanta, Georgia with a full academic scholarship. Grace bought James' grandmother's house and spent most of her time working in the Sugar Shack. She and I spent many evenings talking and reminiscing about our past. Sometimes Grace sounded so much like Aunt Wanda until I would have to look twice to make sure I wasn't dreaming.

My line of clothing was booming. My newest outfits were mini sun dresses with matching shorts. Some were floral, some were stripped, some had polka dots and some were just solid colored. They were selling faster than Mama's candy and ice cream.

Grace said she wanted to buy me an early graduation present. I thought it was going to be a modern sewing machine. When I saw the small box, I knew it wasn't. Inside were two plane tickets to New Orleans.

"I don't understand," I said to Grace.

"One for you and one for me," Grace explained. "I'm taking you to the Mardi Gras. We leave on Friday and return on Monday afternoon."

I could hardly contain my joy. Grace knew that I would get to see James. I was so excited until I forgot all about school. Mama and Daddy knew about the trip already because Grace had gotten their permission to take me. They figured missing one day of school would not be so bad.

Grace and I boarded the plane in Little Rock. We had seats B and C. I was hoping seat A would remain empty so we wouldn't be so squished. One of the flight attendants escorted an old man down the aisle. He was bald in the top with a row of gray hair around the sides. He was tall and, thank goodness, he was thin. Grace and I stood in the aisle and let him slide into seat A. He carried a small book in his hand and he smelled like cough drops.

I'm glad this is a short flight, I thought.

When the plane landed, the stewardess came to help the old man out.

"Sir," she kindly said, "Your escort is here to take you to your meeting."

He smiled at Grace and me and said, "Enjoy your stay here in New Orleans."

Then he held onto the stewardess' arm and went out.

"He's cute," Grace smiled. "I wonder what he looked like when he was younger?"

In my excitement about seeing James, I really didn't care what the old man looked like years age, so I just shrugged my shoulders. As I gathered my things from the seat, I spotted the old man's book on the floor. I held it in my hand, hoping to see him in the baggage claim area, but he was nowhere to be found. The book looked brand new, as if he had not yet read it. I stuck it in my purse and Grace and I boarded the shuttle and checked into our hotel room. Grace seemed very excited.

"Get a good night's rest," she said. "We will be up and out early in the morning."

By the time my head hit the pillow, I was sound asleep.

Grace was not kidding. She woke me up at 4 A.M. Crowds lined the street early for the parade. The sky was dreary and it was quite windy. James used to say windy days and stilt-walking don't go together. Loud, lively music came from the megaphone on top of the decorated car that drove up and down the street before the parade began. People danced and flung white cloths around and around over their heads like lassos. The parade started and everyone yelled and clapped. Everything was so colorful, it almost made my head spin. In the distance I could see the tall stilt-walkers approaching.

"That's James!" I shouted to Grace.

I began to jump up and down. The wind was blowing pretty hard, but I took my jacket off so James could see my cute, yellow blouse.

The closer they got, the louder I screamed, "James! James!"

He heard his name and turned to look. He was so surprised to see me that he lost his balance and fell into the crowd of people. No one was hurt, but James was so embarrassed. His father, who was walking along beside them, helped him get back up and they continued down the street in the parade. I was so exhausted when we returned to the hotel, I laid down and took a nap. When I awoke, I heard Grace talking on the phone.

"I'm sorry to hear that, Mr. Mitchell," she said.

Grace later told me that, because of the accident, the parade commissioner let the stilt-walkers go. I haven't heard from James since then.

On the flight back home, I took the old man's book out of my purse. I had not paid attention to the title. It said, The Mistakes We Make In Life. I quickly stuck it back into my purse. I didn't want to even think about mistakes.

James probably hates me by now, I thought.

I was happy to see Mama and Daddy when we got back home. I couldn't wait to crawl into my own bed that night on my cool, silky sheets. I fell asleep right away.

The morning sun peaking through my curtains, woke me up in time for school. The only person that seemed upset about my absence was my literature teacher.

She said, "Miss Gwen, I will excuse your absence if you can show me that you had a book with you on your trip."

I thought quickly, "Yes," I said, "I had this book with me."

I pulled out the old man's book from my purse.

"Oh," the teacher smiled, "That's a good book. You will like it when you finish reading it. Just make an entry in your journal on your feelings about the book. That will be your grade for the missed day."

I think she knew I had not read it. The book looked too new.

I began reading the book at lunch time. This was just one more thing I had to do on top of everything else. But, I had to do it.

I read the book every chance I got. The setting in the story was Louisiana. The characters were a man and his family. The more I read, the more I realized that there was something very unusual about this story. It sounded like something I had read before.

That evening, as I sat reading in the Sugar Shack, Grace seemed a little sad. I stopped reading long enough to thank her for the nice trip to the Mardi Gras.

"Before I go away to college, I will have to do something special for you." I said.

Grace laughed and said, "Just being my friend is enough."

I hadn't realized that Grace had no other real friends or family that she spent time with.

Maybe I can find her father. I pondered this thought in my mind.

Every day when Grace and I talked, I would ask her something about her father or her family life. I began to write down the things she would tell me. Pretty soon, I had a good collection of information. One thing I noticed was that Grace's story was very similar to the story in the old man's book.

I contemplated contacting the author, hoping that he might know Grace's father. A short autobiography at the back of the book gave a Post Office box where he could be reached. It was in Austin, Texas. Mama and Daddy thought it was worth a try. I wrote a letter and explained my situation.

In a very short time, a response came in the mail:

> *Dear Miss Gwen,*
>
> *I have been traveling quite a bit lately, but I would like to come to Warren for a book signing and meet your friend face-to-face. Maybe her ideas will help me write my next book.*
>
> *Sincerely,*
>
> *Mr. Henderson*

Mama arranged for the book signing to be at the Sugar Shack. I made fliers to advertise his coming. Grace and Mama made plenty of candy and ice cream for the special day.

A shiny, silver-gray car pulled into the driveway on the day of the event. A tall, slender man in a gray suit and tie got out. I almost fell to the ground when I saw that it was the old man from the plane. An escort was with him. He said that because of his poor vision, Mr. Henderson never liked to travel alone. I was totally surprised that the old man was actually the author of the book.

We all welcomed them and showed them where to set up for the signing. I kept staring at Mr. Henderson in amazement.

"Grace is going to be shocked." I whispered to Mama. "This is the man we sat next to on the plane."

When Grace arrived in her royal blue, fitted dress with silver high heels, I smiled and told her how pretty she looked.

Mr. Henderson stood up with a big smile on his face, as if he was looking at a long, lost friend.

I introduced Grace to him and his escort.

"This is Grace Tyler," I said proudly.

"I remember you from the plane!" she said surprisingly, as she shook his hand.

"And what is your name?" Grace asked his escort.

"I'm Eric," he replied.

Grace seemed to be a little uncomfortable, but as the day went on, she seemed more at ease.

Mr. Henderson signed book after book. I took a picture of him and Eric sitting at the table. The thick lenses in his glasses seemed to help his vision greatly.

Finally, Grace gave him a book to sign for her. Before signing, he began to talk to her about his story. As I listened, I noticed that Eric seemed very nervous. Mr. Henderson began to ask Grace questions about her family. The smile on his face gave me the impression that he might know her father. It seemed as if he wanted to have accurate information before writing anything special in her book.

When all of the questions were answered, silence filled the room. Mr. Henderson began to write in Grace's book.

Does he know Grace's dad? I wondered.

If he doesn't, I sadly thought, at least my intentions were good.

He wrote a long message in her book, then gave it to her for free.

We watched as she sat and read the message. She began to weep like she did at Aunt Wanda's funeral.

I handed her a handkerchief as she looked at Mr. Henderson and said, "Daddy, you found me!"

They hugged for a long time. Then Mr. Henderson put his hand on Eric's shoulder and said, "This is your half brother."

Eric began to cry. I was crying, too.

I was trying to make sense out of all of this, so I asked Mr. Henderson about his name. He said that his real name is Henderson Tyler, but he uses Mr. Henderson as his author name. He and Grace had not seen each other since she was nine, so it wasn't a surprise to me that they hadn't recognized each other.

He told Grace about my letter and my desire to find her father.

As I hugged her, I said, "This is your special gift from me."

Grace's father and brother stayed with her for a few days. I've never seen her so happy.

****

I graduated at the top of my class. Grace moved to Texas with her father and brother. She helped her father write his next book, 'Sugar Shack'. It was a best seller.

My first week at Spelman College was the best week of my life. As I sat on the steps by my dorm, I recalled my list of priorities. Mama and Daddy were healthy and financially stable. I was accomplishing my educational goals. Mama and Daddy gave me a modern sewing machine to use to continue my clothing business, and my friend, Grace, was happy with her family. Marriage? Well, that will come whenever the Lord sends the right man.

As I stood up to go back inside, I heard someone calling my name. To my surprise, James came running across the grass.

"Hello," he said. "My name is James Mitchell. I'm a student at Morehouse College. My goal is to graduate at the top of my class, then get married."

We hugged just like we did back home at Mama's Sugar Shack.

"The right perspective," I said.

James took my hand and said, "At the right time."